This book belongs to:

....

....

Quarto is the authority on a wide range of topics.

Quarto educates, entertains and enriches the lives of
our readers—enthusiasts and lovers of hands-on living.

www.quartoknows.com

Author and Illustrator: Steve Smallman
Editor: Harriet Stone
Designer: Victoria Kimonidou

© 2018 Quarto Publishing plc

First published in 2018 by QEB Publishing,
an imprint of The Quarto Group.
6 Orchard Road, Suite 100
Lake Forest, CA 92630
T: +1 949 380 7510
F: +1 949 380 7575
www.QuartoKnows.com

A CIP record for this book is available from the Library of Congress.

ISBN 978 1 68297 381 3

9 8 7 6 5 4 3 2 1

Manufactured in Guangdong, China

CC022018

MIX
Paper from
responsible sources
FSC® C008047

ASTROMOUSE

by STEVE SMALLMAN

QEB

"Look, Mom!" cried Pip excitedly. "I can see a mouse! There's a mouse on the moon!"

"Where?" asked Mom.

"There, look!" insisted Pip.

"Oh, yes," said Mom
(although she couldn't
see anything at all).

"Well, I'm not surprised," she added.
"People do say that the moon is made of cheese."

"Stinky cheese?!" gasped Pip.

Stinky cheese was his favorite meal—ideally with cracker crumbs on top!

"Well, maybe," chuckled Mom.

"Can I live on the moon?"
Pip asked.

"I don't think so, Pip—
it's too far away.
Time to go to sleep
now. I'll see you
in the morning."

But Pip was too excited to sleep. He crept outside. The moon was shining big and bright just above the top of Windy Hill.

"I wonder if it really is made of stinky cheese," thought Pip.

"If I can just make it to the top of the hill and break off a little piece..."

Once at the top, Pip jumped up and down as high as he could, but he still couldn't reach the moon.

"Can I live on the moon today, Mom?"
Pip asked at breakfast the next day.

"You would need to be an
astronaut with a space rocket
to fly to the moon," said Mom.

"What's an as...tro...nut?" asked Pip.

Mom showed him a book with pictures
of rocket ships and astronauts in it.

"Look Mom,
I'M AN ASTROMOUSE!"
cried Pip.
"Can I live on the moon now?"

"But how will you get to the moon, Pip?" asked Mom.
"You don't have a rocket."

"Oh yes I do!" he squeaked excitedly. **"Look!"**

Pip had made himself a wonderful rocket out of an old funnel, sticky tape, and cardboard.

But it didn't seem to want to blast off.

"Perhaps I need a launch pad," Pip thought.

The next day Pip made a launch pad out of a log and an old piece of wood. He left it at the bottom of Windy Hill.

Then he dragged his rocket all the way up to the top using an old roller skate.

Pip climbed into the rocket clutching
a bag full of cracker crumbs (to eat
with the stinky moon cheese).

He was ready for takeoff!

3, 2, 1...

BLAST OFF!

Pip's rocket rolled down the hill...

...faster and *faster*, onto the launch pad...

...up into the
sky and then...

...down again
with a big

BUMP!

Pip's rocket was broken, his space helmet was dented, and his cracker crumbs were all over the floor.

He made his way sadly back home.

Then he saw something shining brightly in a pond.
It was the moon!

"**Wow!**" he cried, "I couldn't get to the moon, so the moon has come to me!"

He crept to the edge of the pond and reached down to break off a piece of stinky cheese.

But the moon didn't smell like stinky cheese.
It smelled like a stinky pond!

Suddenly two big yellow eyes
popped out of the middle of the moon.

"**EEEEEEEEK!**"

squeaked Pip. He ran as fast
as he could, all the way home.

Mom met him at the door.

"Wherever have you been, Pip?"
she cried.

"To the moon," said Pip.

"And I don't want to live there any more.
It's not made of cheese, it smells like a
stinky pond, and there isn't a mouse
on the moon, there's **a frog!**"

"Well, in that case," said Mom, "would you like to live here with me instead?"

Pip gave his mom a great big hug, which of course meant...

...yes!

NEXT STEPS

Show the children the cover again. Could they have guessed what the story was about just from looking at the cover? Did any of the children think it would be a story set in space?

Pip really wanted to live on the moon. Can the children remember why?
Do they think that the moon is really made of cheese?
What food would they like the moon to be made of?

Pip decided to be an "Astromouse."
Would any of the children like to be an astronaut and fly to the moon?
What do they think they would see? How would it feel to be in outer space?

Pip tried really hard to fly his rocket to the moon.
How do the children think he felt when it crashed?

Pip thought that the moon had come down to the pond. What was it really?

Pip decided at the end of the story that he didn't want to live on the moon after all.
Where did he decide to live instead?
What made his home the best place of all?
Ask the children what is special about their homes.

The next time the children see a full moon ask them to look
carefully and see if there really is a mouse on the moon!